I got a Great-Gran, loves me still

(Whisperin' quiet, when she will),
Can't see me comin', but knows I'm there,
Touches my face and pats my hair.
Smiles crackle 'cross her crinklin' lips,

I GOT A FAMILY

by Melrose Cooper
pictures by Dale Gottlieb

Henry Holt and Company · New York

For M.K. and Fath,
my Mamma Daddy
— M.C.

Henry Holt and Company, Inc.
Publishers since 1866
115 West 18th Street
New York, New York 10011

Henry Holt is a registered trademark of Henry Holt and Company, Inc.

Published in Canada by Fitzhenry and Whiteside Ltd.,
195 Allstate Parkway, Markham, Ontario L3R 4T8.

Library of Congress Cataloging-in-Publication Data
Cooper, Melrose / I got a family / by Melrose Cooper / pictures by Dale Gottlieb.
Summary: In rhyming verses, a young girl describes how the members of her family make her feel loved.
[1. Family—Fiction. 2. Stories in rhyme.] I. Gottlieb, Dale, ill. II. Title.
PZ8.3.C788Ig 1993 [E]—dc20 92-1689

ISBN 0-8050-1965-0 (hardcover)
3 5 7 9 10 8 6 4 2
ISBN 0-8050-5542-8 (paperback)
1 3 5 7 9 10 8 6 4 2

First published in hardcover in 1993 by Henry Holt and Company, Inc.
First Owlet paperback edition, 1997
Printed in the United States of America on acid-free paper. ∞

Life oozes out her fingertips.

I got a Grampy, loves me sweet,
Takes me to Frosty's for a treat,

Gives me the cherry right off his dish
And all of his whip-cream, if I wish,
Calls me his Sugar 'n' Pumpkin Pie,
Says I'm the sparkle in his eye.

I got an Uncle, loves me wishin'.

He's got a special place for fishin',
Says that he's shared it just with me!

Hunkerin' under his willow tree
Right where the riverbed meets the streams,
We bait our gear and cast our dreams.

I got an Auntie, loves me teachin',

Takes me out on an expedition

Over the playfield, through the park,

Watchin' the dusk turn into dark,
Hearin' the bats and nighthawks' cries,
And countin' the planets in the skies.

I got a Brother, loves me hard

Roughhousin' in our fenced-in yard,

Teachin' me hoop-shoots at the school

Or swimmin' and floats at the public pool,
Tellin' me things just brothers know
All 'bout our relatives long ago.

I got a Daddy, loves me high,

Swings me in circles in the sky,
Turnin' me into a supersoarer:

I am an outer-space explorer!

Softens my landing, smooth 'n' slow,
Steadies me till the dizzies go.

I got a Mamma, loves me sewin',

Keeps all the hems in my dresses growin',
Lengthens my sleeves when they shrink a bit,
Makes other pants when the old don't fit,
Swirls me in colors, every hue,

Wraps me in comfort all year through.

I got a Kitty, loves me furry,

Weaves through my legs and gets all purry,
Plays whisker-tickle with my face,
Stretches with me in our sunny place,
Mews me a thank-you when she's fed,

Washes up clean when it's time for bed.

I got a Family, lovin' me,

Pullin' 'n' pushin' 'n' shovin' me
Into the paths where I gotta go,

Givin' me all that I gotta know,
Pilin' up feelings in a stack.

And I got a heart that loves 'em back!